To the very real, and imaginative, Llewyn Sylvester.
May you find your Greenland – whatever,
and wherever, that may be. —PS

For my loves, Manny and B. —BW

Scholastic Press
An imprint of Scholastic Australia Pty Limited (ABN 11 000 614 577)
PO Box 579 Gosford NSW 2250
www.scholastic.com.au

Part of the Scholastic Group
Sydney · Auckland · New York · Toronto · London · Mexico City
New Delhi · Hong Kong · Buenos Aires · Puerto Rico

Published by Scholastic Australia in 2022.

The illustrations in this book were created using pencil, oil paints and digital painting.

Book design by Hannah Janzen.

A catalogue record for this book is available from the National Library of Australia

ISBN: 978-1-76097-616-3

Typeset in Mrs Eaves XL Serif Nar OT, Acrylic Hand Sans and Brixton Wood.

Printed in China by RR Donnelley.

Scholastic Australia's policy, in association with RR Donnelley, is to use papers that are renewable and made efficiently from wood grown in responsibly managed forests, so as to minimise its environmental footprint.

10 9 8 7 6 5 4 3 2 1 22 23 24 25 26 / 2

TO GREENLAND!

PIP SMITH & BEAU WYLIE

A Scholastic Press book from Scholastic Australia

Llewyn Sylvester went out for the day
and met a green elephant on his way.
Llewyn said, 'Elephant, where have you been?'
'To Greenland!' she said. 'Oh, the things that I've seen!

Jellyfish lights that swim through the skies,
and hills made of ice-cream that roll on for miles,
cottages made out of hot chocolate pies . . .'

'OH, HUSH!' Llewyn said. 'Please stop telling me lies!'

Llewyn Sylvester got on with his day.
The people wore brown
and the buildings were grey.

Even if Greenland was only a dream,
he wished he was skiing
down hills of ice-cream.

Llew packed his suitcase and walked to the zoo,

where he found Ellie Phant . . .

in an emerald igloo.

‘I’m sorry for doubting your story so far,
I’d love to see Greenland, but don’t have a car.’

'Jump on my back,'
Ellie said, 'don't delay –
we'll want to make friends
and play games on the way.'

'To Greenland!' Llew cheered
as he threw up his pack,
then together they crossed
the Australian outback.

They stopped in the desert to help Camel dig,

swayed in the swamp, singing carols with Pig,

baked by the lake
with Koala and Duck,

but once at the coast . . .

they were

DREADFULLY

STUCK.

‘Can you swim?’ Ellie asked,
and, yes, Llewyn could swim,
but he couldn’t tug Ellie
along with him.

So they turned Ellie's hat upside down for a boat,
and she blew through her trunk, to keep them afloat.

Right out of breath when they reached the equator,
they sprawled on a beach by an old alligator.

'You'll have to turn back,'
he grinned with disdain.
'You're only allowed
to reach Greenland by plane!'

'Are there no other options?'
they asked Gator Keeper.
'We're hoping for something
a little bit cheaper.'

'You can't break the rules!' snapped the scaly old geezer.
'And where are you from, green beast? Show me your visa!'
They paddled as fast as they could from his teeth,
which were gnashing and slashing El's hat from beneath.

Llewyn gasped, ‘Ellie, how did you get there before?’
‘Closed my eyes,’ Ellie shrugged, ‘and then counted to four.’
‘I knew it!’ Llew wailed. ‘Greenland’s not even real!’

But his tears were stopped short . . .

. . . by the sight of an eel.

‘A motoring trunk and a panama hat?
You’ll need a more sensible vehicle than that.
Take this yacht! Sail today! Pay me back interest free!

If, in exchange, you could make room for me?’

They agreed and the three sailed the Indian Ocean.
For six weeks their yacht made a sickening motion,
then docked. As they hurled into brown paper bags
Ellie sighed, 'Aren't you glad we avoided jetlag?'

Stumbling ashore Llewyn yelled, ‘No, I’m mad!
What is wrong with you, El, why are you never sad?
We’ve been travelling for months with no sight of ice-cream –
in a hill, cone or cup, and I’m ready to scream!’

‘You’re right,’ Ellie said,
‘we should turn back around.
I made Greenland up,
it can never be found.’

'Greenland's
not real?' the sales
eel sobbed.
The lights in his
fins flickered out.
'I've been robbed!

All my life I've been selling above market price
in the hope I'd retire to that green paradise!'

'It's alright,' Llewyn said, 'let's go on, let's persist,
we can't quit just because Greenland doesn't exist!'

But how would the three of them know where to find
a country seen only inside Ellie's mind?

Llew looked in El's ears,
and crawled in her trunk . . .

where he spied something green,
and slipped over –

He hit what he thought was a dark, dank junkyard,
then flicked on the light and saw walls of postcards,
showing places they'd been, the desert, the coast,
the ocean they crossed, the new friends they'd miss most.

Llewyn shouted so loud El's eyes started to drip –
'We could build it with friends that we made on our trip!'

Ellie sneezed Llewyn onto the ground.
Every ant, ape and antelope froze at the sound.

Then they crawled on their knees,
and swung from the trees,
and flew in balloons
propelled by bumblebees,
armed with sketches they'd drawn
of El's colourful spiel . . .

. . . which they used as instructions
to make Greenland **REAL.**

Would *you* like to visit the land of your dreams?
Where hats can be boats, and eels sell ice-creams?

I'll turn out the light,
tuck you in, shut the door.

Close your eyes, are you ready?
ONE, TWO, THREE ...

HALF PRICE
ICE CREAM

... FOUR!